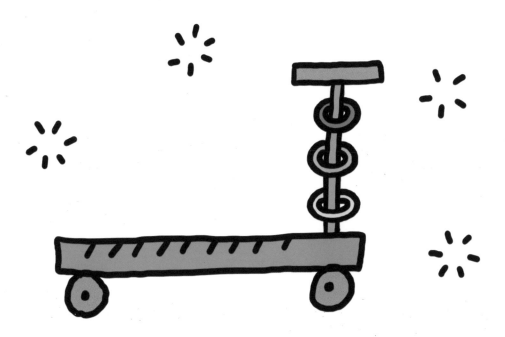

This Faber book belongs to

Joseph Chimkah

ff

FABER & FABER

First published in the UK in 2017
by Faber and Faber Ltd,
Bloomsbury House,
74–77 Great Russell Street,
London WC1B 3DA
Text © Katie Blackburn, 2017
Illustration © Jim Smith, 2017
ISBN 978–0–571–33639–5

Printed in Malta
10 9 8 7 6 5 4 3 2 1

FSC
www.fsc.org

MIX
Paper from
responsible sources
FSC® C022612

# Scoot!

Jim Smith and
Katie Blackburn

# Scooters, scooters, everywhere...

# Do YOU have one?
# Do you dare?

# Watch them go, one by one...

# Scooter mania, ooh what fun!

# Out of the box, shiny and new,

# bumped and crumped and bashed and blue.

Handles full of
rubber bands.

Hey!

Look!

# No hands!

# Covered in stickers,

# flower power!

# Scooter too small.

# Scooter too big.

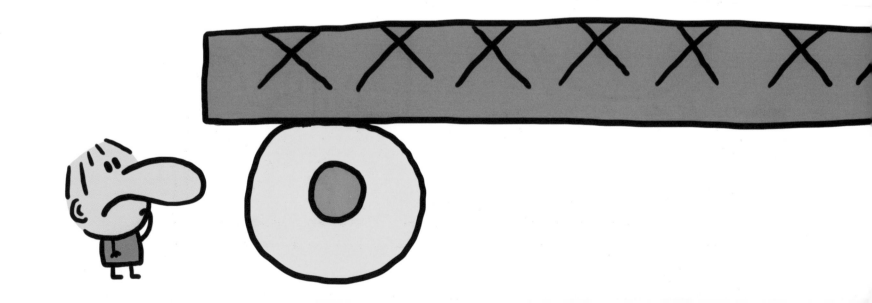

# Family scooter,

# gliding pig!

# Loop the loop,

# up a ramp.

# Whoops, a puddle!

# Clothes a bit damp.

# Jumping, racing, backwards facing!

# Cruising, losing, bit of bruising!

# Stopping, chatting, resting, napping.

# Suiting, booting, back to scooting!

# Scooters, scooters, everywhere!

# Do you dare?